THE ADVENTURES OF LITTLE AL
THE LIE

ALLAN BURD

Illustrated By
LISA LINBRUNNER

BED BUG PUBLISHING, INC. / NEW YORK

To my own Little Al,
Dylan.
- A.B.

The author would like to thank Mark Roselle for his invaluable help in putting this book together. His time and generosity are greatly appreciated.

PUBLISHER'S CATALOGING-IN-PUBLICATION DATA
(Provided by Quality Books, Inc.)

Burd, Allan.
The adventures of Little Al. The lie / Allan Burd ; illustrated by Lisa Linbrunner. -- 1st ed.
p. cm. -- (The adventures of Little Al ; 1)
SUMMARY: Versified telling of how Little Al learns why he should not tell lies.
LCCN 00-192586
ISBN 0-970-55888-0

1. Honesty--Juvenile fiction. 2. Truthfulness and falsehood in children--Juvenile fiction. [1. Honesty.--Fiction. 2. Stories in rhyme.] I. Linbrunner, Lisa. II. Title. III. Title: Lie

PZ8.3.B944Li 2001   [E]
                QBI01-700744

10 9 8 7 6 5 4 3 2 1

Printed in Mexico
First U.S. edition, 2001
The text type for this book was set in 13 point Arial MT Bl.

Al unfolded the map
He saw X marked the spot
There was treasure to find
There was gold by the pot

But the hunt would be tricky
The path fraught with dangers
For the enemies he would meet
Were not kind to strangers

Yet for the famed Pirate Al
No task was too great
He would rise to the challenge
Whatever his fate

1

Cause he was the strongest,
toughest pirate of all
Whom everyone feared
though he stood four feet tall

And together with his sidekick
His trusty dog Zach
They would capture the treasure
And fight back to back

So he rolled up the map
From the floor of his room
Determined to succeed
Where others met doom

He flipped down his eye patch
And withdrew his sword
Let the adventure begin
There was treasure to hoard

2

So together they traveled
to Al's bedroom door
As they peaked through the opening
Was that a giant they saw?

She stood five foot seven
She whistled a song
She carried a basket
She must have been strong

3

Then she turned toward the duo
They ducked back inside
Yet the giant did see them
There was no place to hide

Her voice rang into the room
And it echoed throughout
She had spotted the twosome
She started to shout

"*Little Al*," called his mother
"*I'll need your help when you're done
I'm doing the laundry*"
Little Al cried out "*RUN*"

They zipped out of the bedroom
And ran down the stairs
They escaped their first danger
By the thinnest of hairs

Little Al huffed
as he just caught his breath
*"That one was close
Next time we fight to the death"*

Al unrolled the map
To see what lay ahead
He gasped when he saw
Where the trail had led

For if he had read right
There was trouble around
There were invisible beasts
Stalking this ground

So Little Al said
*"Quickly Zach, guard my back
We are surrounded by monsters
We are under attack"*

Then Al bolted to action
With daring and skill
He fought off the beasts
Oh, it was quite a thrill

The battle was won
His hands did Al raise
But Little Al wasn't looking
And knocked over the vase

The flowers flew out
The vase hit the floor
The adventure was over
Al was a pirate no more

He knew what came next
He was in tons of trouble
It was Mom's favorite vase
She would be here on the double

But as the seconds passed slowly
As he prepared for the clash
Al had suddenly realized
His mom had not heard the crash

Now he had time to think
But what should he do?
Should he just tell his mom
That he didn't mean to?

He knew she would be mad
But what else could he do?
Perhaps he could fix it
With some super glue

He had to do something
Or Mom's wrath he would face
He thought of his punishment
His mind started to race

*"She'll ground me forever
I will be stuck in my room
For a year, maybe more
My life will be gloom"*

9

But then he thought of a way
To escape without blame
He had to think like a Pirate
And live up to his name

Yes, Pirate Al was the best
He had always survived
No matter the odds
He had managed to thrive

Yes, this was the way
Forget about glue
Just think like a pirate
That is what he would do

So the adventure renewed
And Al's smile grew merry
There was no treasure to find
Now there was treasure to bury

So he went to the garage
Got a broom and dust pan
He swept up the pieces
Putting them in a can

He ran through the back door
And into the yard
He buried the can
"Gee, that wasn't so hard"

Al thought himself safe
How clever he had been
He was pleased with himself
He let out a grin

Then with footsteps he crept
Quietly like a mouse
Right through the back door
Back into the house

Pirate Al was the best
He had done it again
Then Little Al's mom
Walked into the den

Little Al's heart sped up
Though he did keep his cool
His mom would not notice
He thought her a fool

For he was Pirate Al
The best of all time
He buried the evidence
He had covered his crime

Then mom looked around
Something wasn't quite right
Her eyes leered about
Her lips closed real tight

She walked around slowly
Something was suspect
Then she did something
That Al did not expect

"*Little Al*," asked his mom
"*Did you see my vase?*"
She looked into his eyes
With that motherly gaze

Now Al was in trouble
For it was one thing to hide
But as long as he lived
He never had lied

But there was no other choice
It was his only way out
"*No I didn't*," he said
But his mother had doubt

14

She looked at the floor
She noticed the dirt
Al brought in from the yard
and had on the sleeve of his shirt

"*I see you were outside
You played in my garden*",
Mom said with suspicion
Her face started to harden

15

She went into the yard
She looked all around
Then went straight to the garden
And studied the ground

Cause something was not quite right
The soil was lumpy
And her son Little Al
Was getting quite jumpy

16

Then she looked even closer
She started to dig
She clawed with her hands
Till she found something big

Then she pulled out the can
Little Al knew this was it
*"Mom, that's my buried treasure
I was playing pirate"*

And just as he said it
He could not believe
That was two lies he told
Just so he could deceive

17

"Well, let's see your treasure"
Then mom poured out the "gold"
Her mouth opened wide
She began to scold

"How could you have broken
My favorite vase
Then hide it from me"
Her eyes were ablaze

"Right here in my garden
What were you thinking?"
Little Al got all flustered
His pirate ship was now sinking

For he had been caught
His mom was irate
He should tell her the truth
But he thought it too late

Cause he had already lied
In fact, he lied twice
He knew deep down inside
That was not very nice

Then he looked into the eyes
Of his very mad mother
And thought his only way out
Was to tell her another

18

"I didn't do it
Zach broke the vase"
Little Al blamed his dog
Who looked on in a daze

"And then I knew you'd get mad
So I tried to save Zach
I gathered the pieces
Buried them here out back"

"Though I knew it was wrong
And I know I've done bad
It was only for Zach
That I had done what I had"

19

His mother held back
Even though she was mad
Then for reasons unknown
She became very sad

Then she got thoughtful
She said *"I understand
Just don't do it again
Or it's you who'll be canned"*

*"Now go to your room
And stay there till dinner"*
Little Al went in a hurry
He felt like a winner

For he did break the vase
And he gave Zach the blame
He thought once dinner was served
Things would all be the same

A few hours passed
In his room did Al stay
He stared at his ceiling
And thought about his day

He knew lying was bad
But he never knew why
And up till today
He never did lie

The vase was a mistake
He did not break it on purpose
And if he did not lie
Things might have been worse

So what was the harm
Little Al thought there was none
Why not tell a lie
If it does not hurt anyone?

The dinner bell rang
It was supper time
Little Al sat in his chair
He was ready to dine

Then mom brought the food
They would eat meatloaf tonight
But something was missing, Al thought
Something wasn't quite right

Al looked all around
Someone wasn't there
"Mom, where is our dog Zach?
He's usually here"

Then Mom answered calmly
"After what happened today
He could no longer stay here
So we gave him away"

"But Mom, how could you do it?
He was my best pal"
"Your pal broke my vase"
Mom told Little Al

"But Dad," Al cried out
"We must get him back
I must have my pal
I can't live without Zach"

Then his dad shook his head
"Son, the answer is no
Zach got too wild
He just had to go"

Then Little Al realized
It was because of his lie
It was all his fault
That he could not deny

He thought the lies harmless
He now knew he was wrong
All lies were harmful
He should have told the truth all along

But he still had a chance
Perhaps there was still time
To tell them the truth
To confess to his crime

"*Mom, I broke the vase
It was me, It was me
I told you a lie
In fact, I told three*"

24

Then Dad looked at Al
He looked right in his eyes
"Oh come now my son
I know you don't tell lies"

Little Al continued to protest
Though it did him no good
He had told too many lies
He was not understood

Cause he told such a good story
In his attempt to deceive
Now that his story was different
No one knew what to believe

Then Al left the table
And went back to his room
His stomach felt empty
His heart full of gloom

25

Little Al went to bed
He tossed and he turned
He could not help but think
Of the lesson he learned

He should not have lied
He should have confessed
Cause though he wasn't punishe
Now he was twice as depressed

Then he thought about Zach
Oh, where might he be?
He could be in danger
And it's because of me

Then at 11:00 at night
Little Al got out of bed
He still could not sleep
With these thoughts in his head

So he went to his parents
They said, "Come on in"
Little Al walked in slowly
with a frown to his chin

"I can't sleep Mom and Dad
Because I did break that vase
It was all my fault"
His mom gave him a gaze

"Then I hid it from you
Because I was afraid
Then I blamed it on Zach
What a big mess I made"

"I deserve to be punished
And not my pal Zach
You can get rid of me
But you must get Zach back"

And the strangest of all
Was the look of Al's dad
He was not angry at all
Instead he was glad

"Come over here son
I have plenty to say
You did a lot wrong
On this troublesome day

You see, breaking the vase
That wasn't so bad
Sure mom would have been angry
She would have been mad

But accidents happen
We would have understood
Cause we know our son
Always tries to be good

28

But when you lied to your mom
knowing the truth all along
Well that was much worse
That was very wrong

Because all lies are harmful
They hurt everyone
They do no good at all
They ruin all your fun

They hurt the people you blame
Just like they hurt Zach
Had he heard what you said
He might not want to come back

They hurt the people you tell
They made your mom sad
Cause she thought she could trust you
Till you lied like you had

29

But the person who hurts
Much worse than the rest
Is the liar himself
Who others detest

Because his lies don't fool any
Everyone sees right through
We can all smell a lie
We can all tell what's true

And when the truth is discovered
When the liar is shown
No one believes him again
Because that is how he is known

So lying is bad
I hope that you can see
The best way to go
Is complete honesty"

And Little Al knew
That his father spoke true
His lies had caused harm
His days of lying were through

*"I'm sorry Mom
I should have known better than
to tell you those lies
I'll never do it again"*

"Apology accepted"
Little Al's mom then said
*"We'll talk more tomorrow
Now go back to bed"*

So Little Al went
His lesson learned well
From tomorrow and on
Only truths he would tell

And after a while
Little Al fell asleep
The night sky took over
There wasn't a peep

Until at 7:00 A.M.
When Al felt a slight kick
His face got all wet
As he was awoke with a lick

He stirred, then he rubbed
The fairy dust from his eyes
Another lick hit him
It was quite the surprise

Little Al's eyes grew wide
He threw his hands in the air
Al was licked two more times
A bark he did hear

33

"Zach's back," yelled Al
He gave his dog a big hug
All was right with the world
His heart felt a tug

"I'm sorry my friend
I did something bad
If you weren't a dog
I'm sure you'd be mad

I'm glad that you're back
And I will tell you this
I won't do it again"
Then he gave Zach a kiss

One week had now passed
Al was out in the yard
On the ground was a map
Of the house under guard

There was treasure within
There was gold to be got
Their map had a big X
That did mark the spot

Though inside would be danger
For the great Viking Al
There was no challenge too tough
For him and his pal

The great Viking Zach
feared no monster or man
He would fight by Al's side
Whenever he can

35

So Al rolled up the map
"Let the adventure begin"
He reached for the door
He was about to go in

Then Al looked at Zach
Through his Viking eye patch
And he drew out his sword
As he reached for the latch

"There be gold in this castle
The treasure is great
And I'll stand by your side
Whatever our fate

But no matter the riches
I've learned this much is true
The greatest treasure of all
Is my friendship with you"

GLOSSARY

ablaze - 1) on fire, 2) excited

confess - to acknowledge or reveal (a fault, crime, etc.)

daze - 1) to overwhelm, 2) to stun with a blow, shock, etc.

deceive - to mislead or trick

deny - to declare that a statement is not true

depressed - sad

detest - to dislike or hate

duo - a couple or pair

evidence - something that shows proof

flustered - nervous

fraught - to be filled with

gasped - a sudden, short intake of breath

gaze - a steady intent look

gloom - filled with sadness

harmless - not able to cause injury or harm

hoard - 1) to take a large amount, 2) a supply that is hidden for future use

invisible - not able to be seen

irate - angry

latch - a device for holding a door closed

leered - to look with a sideways glance suggestive of interest

peep - the slightest sound

protest - an expression of disapproval, or dissent

renewed - to begin or take up again

stalking - to walk with stiff or haughty strides

surrounded - enclosed on all sides; encircle

suspect - 1) to believe to be guilty with no proof, 2) to doubt or mistrust

suspicion - inclined to suspect; distrustful

thrive - 1) to be successful, 2) to develop vigorously

twosome - two people together

withdrew - to move back or away

wrath - punishment or anger